Goblins Ab

HarperCollins *Children's Books*

It was a peaceful day in Toyland. But deep inside the Dark Woods trouble was brewing. The Goblins were up to no good. Gobbo had come up with another naughty plan for causing mischief in Toy Town.

"Um…Gobbo?" asked Sly. "What are we
looking for?!"

"We are looking for Noddy! When he comes
to deliver our package we are going to steal his
car!" answered Gobbo.

"Oh – great plan! Why?" Sly tried again.

"So we can cause trouble in Toy Town,"
replied Gobbo.

"Now get out of my way! Let me look," said Gobbo pushing Sly off the box he was standing on.

"I think Noddy is already here," said Sly.

"Where?" Gobbo asked impatiently. "I don't see anything!"

"There," said Sly, pointing straight up into the sky.

The Goblins looked up into the sky to see Noddy in his aeroplane. Noddy's aeroplane was full of packages. He dropped one in front of the Goblins.

"Sorry, Gobbo," called Noddy. "I've got so many packages that I'm using my aeroplane to make the deliveries quicker."

Noddy gave a final wave and flew away.

Gobbo was angry at not being able to steal the car. But being a rather naughty Goblin, he soon came up with another plan to cause trouble.

"How are we going to steal Noddy's car now, Gobbo?" asked Sly.

"Who cares about the car," said Gobbo, with a grin on his face. "We are going to steal an aeroplane!"

Big-Ears was in his garden when Noddy flew over.

"Noddy must be very busy today," thought Big-Ears. "It's been a while since I've had something delivered by 'air-mail'."

Big-Ears gave Noddy a wave.

"Coming down, Big-Ears!" said Noddy, dropping another package from his aeroplane.

At the airport Mr Sparks was waiting for Noddy to arrive. Mr Sparks was going to do some work on Noddy's aeroplane.

"Hmmm," wondered Mr Sparks, "Noddy is late. He must have had a lot of packages to deliver."

Just then, Noddy flew down to the runway. He jumped out of his aeroplane as soon as it stopped and ran towards his car.

"Hi, Mr Sparks," Noddy said. "Bye, Mr Sparks.
No time to stop. I still have a lot of deliveries to
make. Thank you for working on my aeroplane."

"You're welcome, Noddy," Mr Sparks said,
waving.

Noddy was soon heading towards Toy Town in
his car, whilst Mr Sparks got to work on his
aeroplane.

A little while later, Mr Sparks had nearly finished adding his new invention to Noddy's aeroplane.

"A little twist here and a turn there and… Tah-dah!" Mr Sparks twirled his spanner in the air.

"I hope Noddy will never have to use the new invention," thought Mr Sparks. "But if he does, he'll be glad it's there."

When Mr Sparks left, the Goblins saw their chance to steal the aeroplane.

"Come on, Sly. Let's go!" shouted Gobbo, climbing into the pilot's seat.

"But, Gobbo," said Sly, worriedly. "We don't know how to fly an aeroplane. We could go zooming out of control and cause all kinds of trouble!"

"Exactly!" laughed Gobbo.

Noddy was driving back into town when he met Bumpy Dog.

"Hello," said Noddy, stopping his car. "I can't play with you right now, Bumpy Dog, I'm very busy."

Bumpy Dog looked sad. He wanted to play fetch.

"Woof!" he said.

"Alright," said Noddy, throwing a stick. "But just one time."

The stick flew up into the air and…was caught by Gobbo in Noddy's aeroplane!

"Hey!" shouted Noddy. "That's Bumpy's stick…AND THAT'S MY AEROPLANE!"

"Ha, ha," cackled the Goblins.

"It's our plane now," called Gobbo.

"And our stick," added Sly, nastily.

"Come back with my aeroplane RIGHT NOW!" cried Noddy, as he began to run along after the Goblins.

Bumpy Dog joined in the chase too. "Woof!" he barked.

But the aeroplane was just too high and too fast
for Noddy and Bumpy to be able to catch it.

"I can't hear what Noddy is saying, Gobbo,"
said Sly.

Gobbo smiled, "Then let's go back and ask
him!" he said.

And Gobbo turned the aeroplane around and
began to head towards Noddy!

"Whooa…Help!" cried Noddy, running as fast as he could *away* from the aeroplane.

"Those naughty goblins really have done it this time," Noddy said to Bumpy Dog. "Quick, get in the car. We can go faster if I drive."

Noddy and Bumpy Dog leapt into Noddy's car
and drove off very quickly.

But the Goblins didn't stop chasing them.
Noddy drove to Toy Town faster than he had
ever driven before.

"We are going to have to ask Mr Plod for
help," Noddy told Bumpy Dog.

Mr Plod was busy directing traffic in Toy Town Square.

"Right, let's go. Keep it moving," he said, waving at the cars.

"Mr Plod! Help!" said Noddy, screeching to a halt.

"Why, what's the problem Noddy?" asked Mr Plod.

"The Goblins have stolen my aeroplane,"
shouted Noddy.

"A-ha!" said Mr Plod, thoughtfully. "And where
did you last see the Goblins in question?"

"THERE!" Noddy pointed to the sky.

Mr Plod blew his police whistle and raised his arm.
  "Stop in the name of Plod!" he said, very firmly.
  But the Goblins were not listening. They kept
flying closer and closer to Mr Plod.
  "I said stop! Slow down! Halt!" Mr Plod
shouted desperately.

The Goblins only laughed and kept flying around Toy Town Square.

Dinah Doll had just made some googleberry muffins.

"Hey," she shouted, as the Goblins swooped down and stole them off the tray.

"Hmmm," said Gobbo, licking his lips. "I love googleberry muffins."

Gobbo and Sly had not finished causing trouble yet. They flew over the people of Toy Town, chasing them first one way and then another.

"Whoa," said Mr Sparks, running as fast as he could.

"Help!" cried the Skittle family, as they ducked out of the way.

Big-Ears was watching the Goblins through his telescope.

"Those two are VERY naughty!" Big-Ears thought to himself. "Sly and Gobbo make enough trouble for ten Goblins!"

Luckily, Big-Ears had an idea.

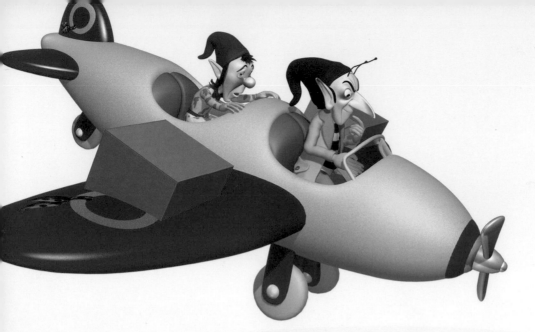

Big-Ears was just leaving his house when the Goblins spotted him.

Gobbo flew towards Big-Ears very quickly.

"Oh, no!" called Big-Ears. "You won't catch me today!"

Big-Ears jumped on his bike.

"Wow! He's pretty fast," said Sly. "For a *gnome!*"

When Big-Ears arrived in Toy Town square Noddy told him what had happened.

"Don't worry, Noddy," said Big-Ears. "I have an idea. When was the last time you put any fuel in your aeroplane?"

Noddy thought very hard. "Not for a long time," he said.

Big-Ears turned to Mr Sparks.

"And have you added your new invention, Mr Sparks?" he asked.

"It's all ready to go," replied Mr Sparks.

"What do we do, Big-Ears?" asked Noddy, slightly puzzled.

Big-Ears calmly replied, "nothing!"

Suddenly the engines on Noddy's aeroplane stopped. They had run out of fuel!

"Yiiiiiiiiiiii!" screamed the Goblins, expecting to fall out of the sky.

But they didn't know about Mr Sparks' invention. The boxes on the wings of the aeroplane suddenly opened and bunches of balloons popped out.

Noddy's plane floated safely to the ground.

Mr Plod was waiting to take the Goblins to jail.

"Oh, thank you, Mr Plod," said the Goblins. "Being in jail is much better than being out of control in the air!"

"And thank you, Mr Sparks," said Noddy. "It is just as well I have friends like you to help. Your invention saved my aeroplane."

First published in Great Britain by HarperCollins Children's Books in 2005
HarperCollins Children's Books is a division of HarperCollins Publishers Ltd,
77-85 Fulham Palace Road, Hammersmith, London W6 8JB

3 5 7 9 10 8 6 4

Text and images copyright © 2005 Enid Blyton Ltd (a Chorion company).
The word "Noddy" is a registered trademark of Enid Blyton Ltd. All rights reserved.
For further information on Noddy and the Noddy Club please contact www.Noddy.com

ISBN-10: 0-00-721059-0
ISBN-13: 978-0-00-721059-6

A CIP catalogue for this title is available from the British Library.

Printed and bound by
Printing Express Ltd, Hong Kong

NODDY™

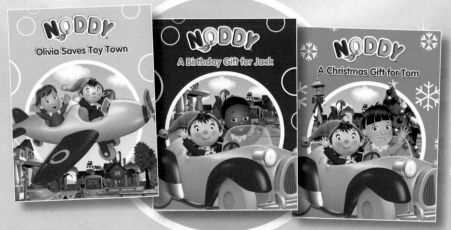